The Starving Time

Elizabeth's Jamestown Colony Diary

· Book Two ·

by Patricia Hermes

Scholastic Inc. New York

Jamestown, Virginia
1609

October 9, 1609

I stand on tiptoe, looking downriver to the sea. In the distance, the ship gets smaller. And smaller. I watch till it is just a blur of white. It goes over the horizon. And drops out of sight.

Gone. It is gone.

I wave.

And wave again.

I turn back to our house. I am trying to be brave. But it is hard because Jessie, my friend, is on that ship. Captain Smith, my friend, is on the ship, too. They are returning to England. And we are left behind here in Jamestown. I have lost so much. I feel angry and black in my heart.

October 12, 1609

I shall tell about this diary. It is my second diary. In my first, I wrote about all that happened here in Jamestown. I wrote it for my twin brother, Caleb, who is in England. Then, when Jessie was leaving, I had a quick thought. Maybe she and her papa and Captain Smith would visit Caleb. Maybe they would take him my journal. Then, he would know all about how we are here. They agreed!

Later, though, I felt sad. My journal was my friend. And do you know? I believe Captain Smith knew my sadness. Just before leaving he sent a sailor to shore in a small shallop. The sailor handed me this book. It is blank pages from the ship's log. Now I have a new journal to keep.

October 20, 1609

I am lonely. I will feel better if I think of this new diary as a friend.

And, it is my friend. I shall write things I would not tell the elders. I shall tell our history and how we came to be here.

But I must do that tomorrow. Tonight, I am so tired. My eyes feel prickly, as though they are filled with sand. I think it was from staring at the ship for so long.

Good night.

October 22, 1609

I promised to tell you how we came to be here. We sailed from England in nine ships last June. We came with hopes for land. Some came for riches.

It was a terrible crossing, and some of our

ships were lost in a hurricane. But our ship, the *Blessing*, came safely to land here in August. I came with Mama and Papa. But Caleb, my brother, my twin, stayed behind in England because his lungs are weak. He will come on the next supply ship in the spring.

We were surprised by what we found here. We must live inside a fort. There are tall, wooden walls that surround us. There are gates that lead to the outside when we wish to go. There are Indians outside. They are friendly some of the time. I have an especially good Indian friend named Pocahontas. She is a Powhatan girl a bit older than me, maybe twelve or eleven. I am just nine. But sometimes our men are cruel to the Indians. And sometimes the Indians do attack. So it is frightening here. Also, there is much sickness and hunger. But there is happiness, too. Our happiest time was when my baby sister,

Abigail, was born. She is the sweetest and prettiest baby ever, though she does squall much.

The worst thing here is being lonely. I miss Caleb. I miss Jessie. There are other children here, but none as dear as Jessie Bolton.

But I am determined to be brave.

I am determined to make myself a new friend.

October 23, 1609

Here is my first secret. I am making a list of people who could be my friends. And — one is named Francis Collier. Yes, he is a boy. I do not like him the way Mary Dobson likes John Bridger. Mary makes eyes at John, though John is a mean and lazy boy. He is so mean, he stole my diary one time. He tried to read it, but I did kick him in his shins. He and Mary even hold hands when they think no one is looking! I would never do that with Francis. I would not do that with any boy. But perhaps Francis could be a friend? I will let you know.

P.S. I just had a thought. I will use a secret code for writing secrets here. Then, if John, or anyone, reads this book, they will not know what I am writing. I will run all the words together. Itwilllooklikethis.

October 25, 1609

Today, something so surprising! Do you recall how I told of Mary Dobson? She is about four years older than me, maybe thirteen. Jessie and I did not much like Mary Dobson. But today, Mary saw me by the well. There is a hidden place in the reeds and grasses there. Jessie and I met there to tell our secrets. I had gone there today to hide. I am afraid that I was crying, for I miss Jessie so. And I long for my brother. Mary Dobson looked straight at me. I thought she would say something mean. But do you know? She touched my shoulder. She said, "I remember. I left my best friend behind in England."

I wonder if perhaps Jessie and I were wrong about Mary Dobson? Do you think I could add Mary's name to my list? I do not know. She thinks too much on boys, it would seem.

October 26, 1609

There is a girl here named Amelia Quick. She is about eight years old, but very little. Her mama died during the ocean crossing, and her papa gets more addled each day. He wanders about, looking for his dear, dead wife. It is very, very sad. Amelia cares for her twin brothers, who are six, and a little baby, Sarah, who is about two. The twins are named Charles and Peter, and they are the most devilish children ever. Today, they almost set fire to the whole fort. They were pretending to be Indians. They used a blanket to make a roof on their Indian dwelling. And then they built a fire — inside of it! The whole thing was burning and smoking. They were crying loudly because they were caught inside. Luckily, Gabriel Archer was nearby and he beat out the flames. He also beat their bottoms! I do not much like Gabriel Archer for his proud, arrogant ways. But I was most happy that he was there today. I also think the twins got just what they deserved.

But do you know? Those boys ran off laughing!

Poor Amelia. She is close to my age. But I do not think she could be a friend. She is much too busy being a mother.

It must be hard to be a mother when you are only eight years old.

October 27, 1609

This Jamestown colony is a hard place to live. Even Mama, who never complains, is weary now, it seems. Since Captain Smith left, we have new leaders. They are Gabriel Archer and George Percy and John Ratcliffe and some others. (I already told you that I do not like Gabriel Archer. I do not much like the others, either.) In just three weeks, they are all squabbling. If one says yes, the others must say no. One wants to eat more food from the storehouse. The others say seal the storehouse till winter! One wants the men to work together for the common good. The others say each man for himself.

There is no one who is a real leader. Who

will keep peace with the Indians? Captain Smith did that before. Who will do it now? Who will bring us food? We are on half rations now.

Papa says I must trust God. I do. But I do not trust Gabriel Archer and George Percy.

October 28, 1609

I have made a friend! And surprise! It is Mary Dobson. She is not the conceited person Jessie and I thought she was. She is not as prayerful and calm as Jessie. But she is very, very funny. She is even sweet.

Today, Gabriel Archer ordered the children to cut weeds by the fences. Some of the little ones were crying, for the weeds cut and tear one's hands. Mary had such a nice way. She worked among the sharp brambles, just like the boys. And soon even the children who cried the most were doing their jobs. They brought their weeds in bundles to Mary, to show how well they had done. She would say, Fine, fine! Such a good job. Their little faces lit up. Even the devilish twins, Peter and Charles, behaved to please Mary.

It makes me a bit ashamed. To think — Jessie and I did avoid Mary Dobson. Just because she likes John Bridger.

I do think I have learned a lesson. I will not judge people before I know them.

October 29, 1609

More about Mary Dobson. She is not at all shy about telling me things. This day, she told me she does have love for John Bridger. She actually said those words!

I think I blushed. Mary just smiled and patted my shoulder. She said, Oh, Elizabeth, someday you will fall in love, too.

Perhaps. But I shall not love someone like John Bridger. He is not even handsome.

October 30, 1609

I must tell you about baby Abigail. She is almost one month old today. Already she holds up her head and holds tight to my finger. She is a strong baby. That is good, because only strong babies can survive here.

At night, I take her out-of-doors to show her the stars. I tell her the names of the winds as Pocahontas taught me. Her eyes get big and wide. She stares into my face.

I think she knows just what I am telling her!

October 31, 1609

Do you know how hard it is to be separated from your twin? Well, this is what I do. At night, I send thoughts to Caleb, my brother, my twin. I pretend that they are little birds, and they fly to him. I send thoughts all about his new sister. I know that he will love her. She will be crawling all about come spring. I tell him we count the minutes till he is with us.

I think that Caleb hears my thoughts.

November 1, 1609

I forgot to tell you. We have a sweet, little house that Papa and I built. It has one big room. There is a curtain across one corner, so that Mama has a private place. It has a window and a fireplace. It is different from England. But it feels almost like a real home now.

Tonight, at twilight, Papa laid a fire on our hearth. Mama was nursing baby Abigail. We talked about Caleb. Just think, Papa said, come spring, Caleb will be here.

That makes me happy. For it will be a real home when Caleb comes.

Good night for now.

November 2, 1609

I will tell you another secret. I know it is wrong of me to hate. But I cannot help it. I hate the Bridger family. Here is why: they are loud and crude and vulgar and very, very lazy. Worse than that, they are just plain mean.

Today, I saw the little Bridger boys, James and Thomas, twirling a frog about by its legs. They twirled and twirled. And then, they flung it hard against the fence. Then, Thomas ran and got it. And they flung it again. They did it again and again.

Oh, I did get boiling angry.

I yelled at them to stop. I ran and grabbed up the frog. But the poor little thing was dead. It was torn apart. Its body lay on the ground in pieces.

Those two boys just laughed at me. Oh, why do I cry when I am angry?

November 3, 1609

Captain Smith was fair to the Indians. And the Indians were fair to us. Now, some of the men here are cruel to the Indians. They steal the Indians' corn and rob their gardens. So the Indians are cruel back. They do not attack our fort. But if our men go outside the walls, they are sometimes killed. Yet we must venture out, for we need to hunt for food.

This morning, four of our men went outside the walls, foraging for food. Now it is night. And not one of the men has returned. One is Master Collier, Francis's father. Tonight, Francis stands on a log peering over the fence.

I do not know what to say to him.

Next morning

The men are still not returned. We are very worried.

November 5, 1609

There is news! Some is good, but some is dreadful. First the good. Two of our men, Master Collier and Master Bridger, have returned! They are injured, but they will live. But the others who went with them are dead. Master Bridger said they were set upon by Indians. He and Master Collier escaped by shooting off their muskets, then running through the forest. But the other two could not run so fast.

And this — when Master Bridger came through the gates, he had an arrow still sticking out of his shoulder!

Mistress Whistler came with her medicine bag. She took the arrow out and bandaged his shoulder. Master Bridger howled like a wolf. We could hear him all over the compound.

Ididnotfeelbad.

November 6, 1609

Food is getting more and more scarce. Today, Papa and the other men huddled in the square, talking. It is only November, and we do not expect a supply ship till spring. So we must have a plan for keeping us through the winter.

Even though we have been on half portions, still, the storehouse is almost empty. Yet there is much food in the fields and woods and the river. But we cannot get to it if the Indians attack.

I hope the men will somehow improve our condition. I am hungry most of the time now.

November 7, 1609

I am very hungry today. All we have eaten for two days is a bit of hardtack and some cornmeal. This morning, the cornmeal was crunchy with bugs. I tried not to notice. But it was hard not to gag.

Papa noticed. He laughed and told me that it was good and nutty!

I know he was trying to make me cheerful. But it is hard to feel cheerful. It is hard to feel anything but hunger. All I think about is my stomach.

November 8, 1609

Remember the Bridger boys? And the frog?
IfIhadthatfrogIwouldeatit.
I am that hungry.

November 9, 1609

Yesterday, Francis Collier came by. He is such a cheerful boy. He always has a friendly word. Even when folks are sick or arguing, he makes things better with his nice ways. I was trying to forget my empty belly. I was busy making a tiny set of dishes — plates and bowls and cups — out of acorn shells. All the acorns have been eaten, but there are many shells on the ground. Some are flat, and some are round. They will make fine doll dishes, though I do not know if I will ever have a doll again. Maybe I shall give them to Abigail when she is bigger.

Francis sat beside me to help. As he shaped the tiny cups with his knife, he began a story. He told of elves and fairies who would use these plates. But before we knew it, we were both talking about food — food, food, food. We talked about porridge and meats and jams that we would put in the bowls and cups.

I know there are more things to think of than food. But I do not know what those things might be.

November 10, 1609

Mama says I talk too much and too fast. And sometimes I say foolish things. I do try not to speak foolishly. I do. But, really sometimes words just jump into my brain. And before I can stop them, they leap from my mouth. As with this: Today I was scrubbing a pot with sand when Mistress Bridger came by. Mistress Bridger was once very, very stout. And selfish and mean, too. But no one here is fat any longer. (She is still selfish and mean though.) She stood looking at me for a long time. I felt my neck get hot. She was going to scold me for something, I knew. Finally, she asked what I was doing.

Well, could she not see what I was doing? I was cleaning a pot. So, very sweetly, I said: I am painting a picture on the bottom of a pot.

Oh, I know I was disrespectful. But it pleased me to be so. I think perhaps I am really a wicked child. And that is exactly what Mistress Bridger said. Then she went to tattle to my mama and papa.

Later

Papa rarely raises his voice in anger at me. He just becomes silent. Then I know that he is disappointed in me.

Tonight, he is very quiet with me.

Iamstillnotsorry.

November 11, 1609

Today, I was drawing water at the well. Mary made a motion for me to follow her to our hidden place. There, she told me something. It surprised me so, I could not speak. Me! Truly, I could not speak. Well, just for a moment, I could not.

Mary said she does wish to marry John Bridger. But she is just thirteen years old. She asked what I thought.

I think she is far too young, though she will

soon be fourteen. But I did not say so. I could see she wanted me to be happy for her.

Then she told me that she had given her blue hair ribbon to John. It is a secret gift. He can hold it and feel close to her. Again, she asked me what I did think.

I could not tell her the truth. But I shall tell you. I think I would rather be a spinster woman my whole life than marry John Bridger.

ActuallyIwouldratherdie.

November 12, 1609

We are all hungry all the time now. Yet at supper time, Papa says he is not hungry. He puts what little food he has onto Mama's plate. She shakes her head. She says she is not hungry. She puts her small portion of porridge or dried meat on my plate.

I try to refuse. But I am ashamed to say — I

gobble it up. I am so hungry. I believe even Abigail is not getting enough when she nurses. How can she? Mama is so thin. Abigail wails all the time now. She seems not as strong. Her cries are sad and weak.

Later

Tonight, Abigail cried and cried. I took her in my arms. I carried her out-of-doors and walked around our house. I tried to show her the stars. You know how I told you she listens to me? Well, tonight she would not listen or look. She kept her eyes pinched closed. She howled and cried and cried. I tried everything. I talked to her. I sang to her. I talked some more. I rocked her. Finally, I gave her my knuckle to suck on. She stopped crying long enough that I could rock her to sleep. I laid her in her cradle. But she whimpered all night in her sleep. It is morning now, and I still hear her pitiful cries.

November 13, 1609

I am scared. Terrified. But excited, too. This is what has happened. Tomorrow morning early, Papa is going to go out to the forest for food. He says he can no longer bear to see us so hungry.

When he said that, Mama cried, No! She said rather he should see us hungry than we see him dead. But, Papa, even though he is quiet and mild, is stubborn. Once he has made up his mind, it is hard to change it.

Well, I made up my mind, too. I said, I shall go, too.

Mama said no.

Papa said no.

I said, While Papa fishes or digs, I can be his

eyes. I can watch for Indians or wolves or bears. I can call out and warn. I said I could even shoot a musket if I must.

Papa and Mama looked at one another. Later, Papa said mayhap.

I pray they will let me go. I know I can help. I just know it.

Later

It is time for bed. They have still not said if I may go. Oh, I wish and wish that they will say yes. I do.

November 14, 1609

It is barely light. Papa and Mama still sleep. Only baby Abigail is crying weakly. She no longer howls.

I have slept with all my clothing on. I have

only to pull on my shoes. I plan to be ready
when Papa is about to go. Maybe if he sees me
dressed he will allow me to go.

I am not afraid.

Well, Iamonlyalittleafraid.

Later

I am to go! Mama is terribly frightened.

I told her we shall return. I said it strongly. I
wish I had a chance to tell Mary. But there is
no time. I know she wishes me well.

Night

It is night. We are returned safely. I have so
much to tell. But I am so tired that I can hardly
hold this pen. I shall write more tomorrow.

November 15, 1609

Return we did. We saw no Indians. And we brought food! We brought enough to feed us for days and days. Papa caught three enormous fish. He dug mussels and clams. And as I sat on the ground keeping watch, I swept a branch beneath the tree. There I found dried corncobs with corn still on them! I found acorns, too. We shall soak them and roast them. Tonight, we shall have a feast. Imagine. Food. Much, much food!

Night

Oh, what a feast! For the first time in weeks I shall fall asleep with my stomach full. We ate roasted fish. We ate corn soup with acorns. We ate some mussels and crabs. Mama was careful not to use it all, though. She has saved a great portion for the coming days. But this day she let us eat till all three of us were full. And with what we have saved, I believe it will be many days, maybe weeks, before we are hungry again.

Even baby Abigail seems contented tonight. Mama soaked a rag in corn soup and gave it to Abigail. Abigail sucked on it all night long. I did not hear her whimper even once.

November 16, 1609, morning

Oh, I am so angry, I could boil. While we slept, a thief crept into our house. This morning, our fish stew is gone! Our corn soup is gone! The iron pot is there. But it is empty. And I know the thief was someone of the Bridger family. Papa says that I cannot know that for sure. But I can. Their lean-to is beside our house. When I awoke early to write in this journal, I saw them huddled about their fire. They were eating silently. The sun was not even yet up. And I smelled the fish.

The Bridgers are even more mean and hateful than I ever did think before.

Papa says that perhaps it is our fault. He says perhaps we were wrong not to share our dinner. He tells me not think harshly of them.

But I do.

Ihopethefoodpoisonsthem.

November 17, 1609

Thankfully, Mama had put the mussels and crabs in a big crock in the fireplace. The thief did not find them. So there is some food at least. But this morning, Mama's eyes are flat and angry.

And I am promising myself that I will find revenge.

Is that a sin, do you think?

November 18, 1609

The men huddled in the marketplace today. They look grave. Some are very angry. I believe everyone knows that the Bridgers are thieves. Some men wished to turn them out and make them live outside the fort. They would not survive a single day out there.

Mr. Percy is one who wanted the Bridgers sent outside. But Papa has a calm way. He would not allow that. His words prevailed. He told me later that we cannot allow thieves. But we must also show mercy. Each man, he says, deserves a second chance.

I believe that is true. But the Bridgers have had second and third and one hundred chances.

November 19, 1609

Everyone is still talking about the Bridgers and their thieving ways. How can people act as they do? They do not work, yet they steal from others who do work. And there is something else. We have lived here three whole months. Papa and I have already built a house. The Bridgers still live in their mean little lean-to.

They are not only thieves. They are lazy thieves.

Ihopebadthingshappentothem.

November 20, 1609

I am sad for poor Mary! Today, she said that she did not care what awful things Master Bridger did. She loves John. She sent a message to him. She plans to meet him tonight behind the well. But girls of Mary's age are not permitted to be alone with boys. So she asked if I would act as look-out. I did not know what to say. She is my friend. But I thought of our stolen food. Perhaps John did not steal it. But did he not eat what his father stole? I also remembered how he tormented Jessie and me and stole my diary. But Mary's eyes were sad. So I told her, yes, I would go.

I am uneasy, though. Mama will punish me if we are found out.

Next day

Mary waited and waited. I looked and looked. But it became dark, and John did not come to the well. He is nowhere to be seen this morning. Mary is afraid that he is hiding from her in shame.

I did not say what I thought — that he *should* be ashamed.

November 22, 1609

This morning Mary came to me. She said this: I do not care at all about John Bridger.

She tossed her head. But her eyes were red from weeping.

And then she told me this. Remember about the blue ribbon that she did give to John? Well, this morning, she saw that the Mistress Bridger sports a blue bow in her matted, gray hair.

Now we both hate the Bridger family.

November 23, 1609

Papa has made a sling kind of thing, as we have seen among some Indians, for my back. Abigail rides there, like a tiny Indian child. But she is a very silent child now. She hardly ever cries. She just sucks silently, her whole fist in her mouth. Oh, I think she is starving!

November 24, 1609

I wonder why Pocahontas no longer comes to our town. She was a great friend to Jessie and me. But she has not been here since Captain Smith did leave. I miss her. She brought laughter. And the Indians did not attack when she was here.

I wonder if she will ever come back.

Later

I have been thinking. Perhaps I shall go to the mouth of the river to visit Pocahontas. I remember the way, for I did go there with Papa and Captain Smith. All I need do is follow the river. I do not believe the Indians would attack a lone child in the woods. Perhaps Pocahontas does not know how hungry and sick we are.

I need to think about this plan.

November 25, 1609

Nights are so cold. And we are more hungry than I ever thought we could be. We have taken to eating everything. A skinny dog has lived in our compound for months. Last week, he disappeared. We all know that he has been eaten, though no one knows who ate him.

In England, that would make me sick to think. But I do not think that sick right now.

November 26, 1609

Last night it rained. It was our first rain in many weeks. It is mild and sunny this morning, almost like springtime in England. The ground is wet, and worms have crawled out to sun themselves. I was sitting on a log beneath a tree writing in this journal. And then I saw this: Mama came out of our door. I saw her bend down. She picked up a worm. She looked around. She did not see me sitting here, but I did see her. She put the worm in her mouth. I watched her chew. And swallow. And chew and swallow. And then she bent and picked up another worm. That, too, went in her mouth. And oh, she was smiling! I had to turn away. She is so hungry! We are all so hungry. But to eat a worm!

I am more afraid than I ever thought I would be.

November 27, 1609

It is so odd. When there is food, I do not think about it much. When there is none, I think about it all the time. But now, now I must tell happy news. And yes, it is about food! Master Collier went outside the gates all by himself. He told no one he was going — not even his poor wife. She was half frantic when she found him gone. He was gone three whole days. But when he came back, he carried a huge leg of a bear. And, he says, the rest of the carcass is off in the woods. It was too heavy to bring in alone.

Meantime, there is enough food here for many. And Master Collier has offered it to anyone who wants to partake. It is to be roasted today, and we will feast tonight.

Papa says that it is the right thing to do. He repeats that we were wrong not to share our fish and corn. From now on, says Papa, we must pray that God will give us generous hearts. I do not know if I can have a generous

heart. But I am very glad that Master Collier
has one.

Later

Oh, how good it is to have food. My
stomach no longer governs my brain. I can
think of other things now. Like this: Mary no
longer talks about marrying John. She told me
yesterday that he is a big hog.

But it makes me sad. I know she has a
hurting place inside of her.

November 28, 1609

Remember how I told you that the men
argue now — and no one seems to know how
to rule? Well, today they were gathered in the
marketplace. I saw John Ratcliffe and Papa

and Master Collier and Gabriel Archer and Master George Percy. Their voices were loud and sharp. Then, I saw Papa raise his hand, asking for silence. He spoke, but I could not hear what he said. The men became silent and somber and they nodded. I know they are planning something, but I do not know what. I wonder if they plan to try to leave this fort. Maybe they will make peace with the Indians. I surely hope they do. Winter is coming. Food will be even harder to find.

Papa is very smart. If there is a plan, it will be a good one.

November 29, 1609

Something good! Papa organized the men into a search party. They went off into the woods. And they did bring back the rest of the bear! It was cut and portioned out to each family. There are about a hundred families left here. Some people argued and wanted more than their share. But, for once, George Percy took charge. He gave the same amount to each family. Most hurried back to their homes to cook and eat it. But one man I saw was eating the meat raw! He must have been near starving.

Papa says there is enough meat for us now to last a long time. I asked for how long. Papa just said, Long enough.

I wonder how long is long enough.

November 30, 1609

How different the world looks when the sun is shining. And one's belly is full.

Today the sun is shining. And my belly is full. So again I can talk of other things. Like this: Yesterday, many of us children gathered at the well. We were all just so happy to feel full in our bellies. There was some good-natured playing and laughing. Even the Bridger boys seemed nice enough. Francis Collier was playing with a hoop toy that one of the children had brought on ship. Then, little Amelia tried to draw up water from the well. But she is so small, she could not lift the bucket. I bent to help her. And when I straightened up, I found little Thomas Bridger trying to peek up under my petticoat!

I grabbed him by his collar and I cuffed him on his ears.

He ran off howling. He said that he would tell his mama.

I hope he does. Then I shall tell Mistress Bridger what I do think. That her son is a miserable rat of a child.

Later

Oh, it is a lovely day. Now listen to this: Mistress Bridger came to complain about me. She told Papa and Mama that I had struck her poor son. Papa asked me if that were true. I said yes. I did strike him. But I was too shy to tell Papa what Thomas had done. My face flamed hot. I whispered it to Mama.

And then do you know? Mama told Mistress Bridger that her son deserved to be walloped.

Mistress Bridger put her hand to her heart. She sat down hard. She looked as though she were about to faint.

It was hard not to smile.

December 1, 1609

The days get shorter and colder. Soon, Christmas will be here.

What kind of day will Christmas be? Will we have Christmas dinner? Will there be gifts? I think not, for what gifts can be found here? I would not mind having a hair ribbon or a hoop toy. But the best gift would be food. I think there will be nothing but prayers this Christmas.

December 2, 1609

I am amazed how much enjoyment I have with Mary Dobson. She chatters as much as I do. We can talk for hours and hours about little or nothing. And everything. Today, we made plans together. No matter how hungry we are on Christmas Day, we said, we shall have a Christmas. Perhaps we can have presents. Together, we shall figure out how to do that.

December 3, 1609

Mary and I have walked all about the fort, looking for things to make — something. Anything. I showed Mary the set of acorn dishes. But we think they be too tiny for Abigail to have yet. So what shall I make for her? And Papa? And Mama?

Then I had an idea. When Jessie's papa took down his lean-to, he left some things behind. There are bits of canvas from an old tent. Mary says perhaps we can make something from the canvas. We shall put our heads together and see what will come of it.

December 4, 1609

Nights are very cold now, and we have had our first snow. And with the snow comes disease. Many, many people have fallen ill. It is almost as bad as it was in the heat of summer. Then, the summer sickness killed so many. There is an open shed, a sick house. This week, the men have covered it with branches and a layer of canvas against the cold and snow. It is once again filled with sick people.

Mama goes there to tend the sick. She has said I may not come. Instead, she leaves me to care for Abigail. She does not want Abigail to be near so much illness.

But I worry for Mama. Will she catch the sickness? She seems frail and she coughs.

Later

Just a little of the bear meat left. Mama added more water to the broth. She left me here to tend it over the fire while she went to the sick house. I wish to go, too. I want to see

Mary. We have much work to do if we are to have gifts before Christmas. But we never leave the house alone any longer. For there are thieves about who will steal one's food. And not just the Bridger family.

December 5, 1609

Mary and I have come up with a plan. We shall sew some bits of canvas into little bags. Then, we shall sew flowers or leaves onto the bags. They can be used for keeping things — Mama's pincushion, perhaps, or a sheath for Papa's knife. And for Abigail, I shall stuff the bag with pine needles. I shall tie it near the top to make a head. I can paint a face on it. It will be her very first doll. It will smell so sweet.

Mary and I have worked feverishly all day.

Oh, what joy it is to have surprises! I can picture the pleasure on Mama's face already!

And perhaps Papa will stop looking worried. He is so distracted these days. He has not called me Sweet Beth in weeks — his special name for me. Some days, he seems not to even notice me. He will notice when I give him his gift.

December 6, 1609

Oh, such dreadful news. Remember that I told you about tiny Amelia Quick? Well, her baby sister, Sarah, has died. She was well enough. And then she was dead. It happened so fast. And now the scary part: Amelia will not let us bury Sarah. All this day she has walked about with Sarah held tightly in her arms. It frightens me terribly.

I hug Abigail even tighter. I put my finger in some thin soup and give her my knuckle to suck on. I have cried for the whole day.

December 9, 1609

Today Papa wrapped his arms around Amelia and her dead baby sister. He rocked her to and fro. He whispered some things to her. We do not know what he said. But she let him take poor little Sarah.

Papa and the men then quickly dug a grave for her in our burial ground. Reverend Harper said a few words. But burials are so common now, no one spends much time praying. Perhaps we pray more inside our own heads. I know that I do.

December 10, 1609

Now, Amelia has become my shadow. Everywhere I go, it seems she is half a step behind. She seems not aware of her wild twin

brothers. I feel like a big sister must feel —
sometimes happy to have her. Sometimes
wishing she would go and leave me be. I
cannot write in my diary but that she asks what
I have written. I cannot draw a picture but that
she breathes over it.

Today, I was working on my acorn dishes.
I sometimes pretend they are a gift to me.
Amelia sat beside me. She picked up each
bowl and cup, turning them over and over in
her tiny hands. I know she feels lonely. So I let
her be. But when she left, a bowl and a cup
were missing.

Perhaps I just dropped them and will find
them in the field in the morning.

December 11, 1609

Today, John Ratcliffe and some of the men
have decided to leave the fort. They plan to go

to bargain with the Powhatans for corn. We are hopeful and we pray for them. But other men will also leave. They wish to make a new settlement farther upriver. They think if they go inland along the water, they will have food and game more easily. But how will they build a fort before winter comes down hard? Already we have had snow. Where will they find enough wood and food and supplies? Can they make friends with the Indians who dwell there?

Master Bridger is the ringleader. He is the one who plans to make his own settlement! He will take his horrid, mean boys with him.

Papa says the Indians will not like the men taking more of their land. And perhaps they will attack the Bridger party.

Idonotcare.

December 12, 1609

I have looked everywhere for my lost acorn dish and cup. Perhaps I dropped them and a squirrel took them. There are few squirrels about, though. If one appears, it is quickly caught and cooked. So where are my tiny dishes?

December 14, 1609

Well, more news. Today, the party set out. But Master Bridger did not take his family with him. He says he will return for them when their new dwelling is complete. I do not blame him for leaving them behind. I would leave them behind, too! We have allowed them food for three days. It is all we could afford to give. Even so, says Papa, there is nothing left in the storehouse.

I do not mind at all that Master Bridger is gone. I cannot wait till he comes back for those loutish boys.

December 15, 1609

Today, Papa and I went to the Colliers' cabin. They need to patch their roof, for it leaks awfully. Francis and I climbed up to help, but first, I tied my skirt like pantaloons.

Francis is such good company. And we work well together. As we worked, Francis told stories, for he is a very fine storyteller. His stories are always about food. Today he told such a story, I could taste the food. He had roasted duck on our plates. He made us breads and butter and duck drippings and root vegetables and corn puddings. Oh, I felt I was in heaven. And then, Mistress Collier did shout up at him. She said, This is not conversation that we can bear!

We finished our work in silence.

December 16, 1609

I can hardly write. I am sick. I have the flux. It is awful. And embarrassing. Mama says perhaps it is from the crabs. We kept them too long. We hope that it is the crabs. We hope it is not the disease that is causing so many to die. I feel as though I shall die.

Night

Baby Abigail is so sick! So it is probably not the crabs. Mama is sick, also. Only Papa is still well. He cares for us. He brings me broth, about the only food we have now. He calls me Sweet Beth. That makes me feel a bit better.

Still, I feel as though my insides have been turned out.

December 17, 1609

Everyone is sick! And sicker. It is sweeping over the whole fort. Papa brought word from the Dobsons. Mary is as sick as she can be. I wish I could go see her. But I cannot. I cannot even stand.

December 18, 1609

I am a tiny bit better tonight. But so weak.

December 19, 1609

Remember how I said I was thinking up a plan? I lie here still weak, but my thoughts run away with me. And this what I think: I think I should go find Pocahontas. She befriended us at the fort. She brought gifts. Maybe it is because Captain Smith is gone that she no longer comes. But if she knew our illness and hunger, would she not help us? I believe she would.

Her father, Chief Powhatan, was good to me. I am close in age to his daughter. Perhaps if I go, he will again share food and gifts with us.

December 20, 1609

I told Papa my thought about Pocahontas. His voice got very stern. He said I must not even think it. The Powhatans are angry with us. It is not safe to approach them now.

Inside my head, I shout: But it is not safe here, either, Papa! We are dying of sickness and hunger.

Later

I have never disobeyed my papa before. But Iamthinkingaboutitnow.

December 21, 1609

I recover slowly. And have a bit more strength. Mama is much better. But her cough lingers on. Baby Abigail is very weak. Mama went to see the Dobsons. She brought me a message from Mary.

It is this: *I think that I might live. Will you?*

I sent a message back. I said, *I am just a tiny bit alive.*

Later

Just when everything seems most bleak, there is a break. A party of eleven men have left to go hunting. They think they shall be safe, for no one has seen any Indians in weeks. We think perhaps the Indians have left for their winter grounds.

The men will also look for the Bridger party and for John Ratcliffe's party. They have not been heard from in weeks.

To help keep the hunting party safe, they have taken some young boys with them. Francis Collier and John and Thomas Bridger go. (Writing the names of the Bridger boys almost makes me gag.) The reason the boys go is so they can climb trees. They will see danger from up high. They can also see game — deer, perhaps, or even bears.

Our spirits are lifted. Though I worry about this: Papa is going with them.

I pray for their safe return.

December 22, 1609

They have been gone for a whole day and a half a day. More and more people are sick. There must be fifty people lying on pallets in the sick shed. Five died overnight. Mama works so hard to help, I fear that she will fall ill again. Even her face is thin.

Baby Abigail is weak. She does not cry. She just stares at me now.

And Papa has not returned.

December 23, 1609, morning

Today, Mary and I tried to stop thinking about our bellies. We pretended to have a big dinner. We came up with a list of words to say how we felt.

Here is our list:

Full
Stuffed
Satisfied
Satiated
Replete
Happy!

ButIamstillhungry.

December 23, 1609, night

Just a quick word. Papa and the men are back! They brought fish. Not much, for the river is frozen. But it is food. We are so happy. They did not meet up with a single Indian man. But they also have not found the Bridger party. And there is a rumor about that John Ratcliffe and his men have been slaughtered. We fear that all are dead.

I will write more after we eat.

Later

We have eaten a bit. Some fish. A handful of dried berries. And saved much.

December 24, 1609, morning

Just that bit of food has made me so much stronger. All day, Mary and I worked on our canvas bags. I sewed a tiny leaf on one and a sprig of pine on the other. They are very pretty. Though I must say, I am not very good with stichery. Oh, you should just see the terrible, rough stitches. But it is hard to sew canvas. I could have painted the bags red with my very own blood, I stuck myself so many times. But they are finished. And Mama and Papa will be happy.

The doll is the sweetest thing ever. I stuffed it full of pine needles. I painted such a sweet,

sweet face for it. I used the ink that I do use here in my journal. It is a smiling face with big eyes and long eyelashes. Abigail will love it when she is well again.

I also made a surprise for Mary. I tore off a bit of ribbon from my petticoat. I washed it and laid it in the sun to dry. Then I sewed it to a tiny square of canvas along with a dried flower. It will make a pretty picture to brighten up her house.

Christmas Eve in the night, 1609

The church bells rang at midnight. It was the first time in weeks that we have heard them. I think folks are too weak to think about prayer service. But it was good to hear the chimes.

The first thing I did upon awakening was send thoughts to Caleb. I sent them on bird wings, and wished him a joyous Christmas. I told him I could not wait till he joins us come spring.

Christmas night, 1609

Papa and Mama had gifts for me! Papa made me a tiny whistle from a reed. He showed me how to play a tune on it. It will take much practice. Mama gave me a slender red ribbon. She had brought it from England, and had saved it for me all this time. I shall lay it across these pages, to mark my place.

Mama hugged me when I gave her my gift. Papa cried. But I knew they were happy tears.

Mama also had a small meal for us, more food than we have had in a while. We had a thin fish broth, and a bit of dried cornmeal made into patties with roasted acorns.

There is only one thing that made me sad

today — Baby Abigail. She can hardly hold up her head any longer. She does not cry. She does not grab and hold my finger. Today, she would not even look at her doll. I held it out to her. Her eyes seemed dull and glassy.

The New Year, January 1, 1610

Oh, the most awful thing.

Today, I went to my hidden place by the well. I was praying for good things that this new year might bring to us. Suddenly, Mary came and sat down by me. Her eyes were red from weeping. I thought at first it was that mean John Bridger. But then she told me — her mama was dead! Just like that. At supper, her mama said she felt unwell. And then she lay herself down. And she died.

What kind of illness could strike so fast?

I did not know what to say. I looked at Mary.

And then I put my arms around her. She cried in my arms like a baby.

I cannot write more.

Winter. Maybe February

Men are leaving the fort — and women, too. They just wander off some days, and do not come back. It is said that some have gone to live with the Indians. But we do not know that for a certainty. And, perhaps, some have been killed by Indians or by wolves.

Our numbers are smaller and smaller. We wonder when the supply ship will come. We know it cannot cross the ocean in winter. We have many months to wait till spring.

Again, February, I think

There is no longer anyone in charge. There are no meetings. There are no workdays. There is nothing of our common life. Just us. Hoping to make it to spring. Hoping to make it till the supply ship comes.

I am hoping to make it till Caleb comes.

I do not know how long we can go on.

Next day

I have not seen Mary in many, many days. I have also not seen Francis. Mama says Francis lies ill in the sick shed. She will not let me go to him. She is afraid that the sickness is catching.

Also, Mary has not recovered well from her illness nor her mother's passing. She sends me messages, though, through Mama. She tells me she misses me something awful.

I miss her, too. She is the happiest thing that has happened to me since Jessie left.

A cold, cold day

Today, I came upon a stranger standing by the well. It was a girl, a very, very thin girl. For one wild moment, I thought: Pocahontas! But, of course, Pocahontas is not thin and frail.

And then the girl turned to me.

It was Mary! But she is so thin, so wispy-looking, that I truly did not recognize her for a moment.

We fell into each other's arms. It was so good to see her again. Right away, we began talking. We talked and talked and talked.

I feel so much better tonight. Talking to a friend makes you feel full up. It is almost as good as having food to eat. But not quite.

February, sometime; very, very cold

No one has seen George Percy or Gabriel Archer for weeks. And we know now that John Ratcliffe has been killed. We think the Bridger party is lost. We also think perhaps our leaders have gone off to the woods. Nobody has the strength to care much at all.

Later

Baby Abigail is dying. I see it in her eyes. It is the look I have seen in so many just before they die.

I shall not let her die!

I shall go to see Pocahontas. I do not care if I die. I only care if Abigail dies.

DoyouthinkIamverybad?

Next day

I have decided.

I shall go to the Indian village and find Pocahontas. I know it is disobeying Papa. He will be very angry.

I shall talk with Mary. She will help me, I know.

Later

Mary knows my resolve. She will help me. I have been hoarding my supper, the bits of bread. I have not eaten in two days. But I have found some pine root that gives some juice when I chew on it.

In the morning, I shall set out. I shall take nothing but my bits of bread and my diary, my friend, and my quill and ink. I shall follow the river.

If I am not back by night fall, Mary will tell Mama and Papa what I have done. We know that they will be angry. They may be angry at Mary.

When I said that to Mary, she just tossed her head. She said, So be it. But I think it worries her. Odd, but I am not afraid tonight.

I am only sad for being disobedient.

Late at night

Mary saved her bit of bread for me, today's portion. She brought it to me tonight. Tears just sprang to my eyes.

Mary laughed. Silly one, she said.

I need hope now. And strength. And maybe forgiveness.

Next day

I crept away early, before the sun was up. All day, I followed the river. I walked softly, praying to avoid Indians. But at times, I have felt eyes watching me. I hear a soft footfall. I stop. The footsteps stop.

Once, I heard an owl call. But it was broad daylight. Owls do not call in the day. I am sure it was an Indian call.

Now it is getting dark. I have found a small cave in the side of a hill. Inside, I feel somewhat safe. I draw myself to myself, making me as small as I can be. The forest is so still. The only thing I hear are leaves falling, it is that quiet. A bird hoots in the brush. My heart beats so loudly, I fear it can be heard.

I believe I am becoming ill again. I feel hot and then cold. I am very, very shivery even with my shawl wrapped around me. But maybe that is just fear? Oh, have I done something truly foolish?

Morning

The sun is shining. I have slept all through the night. And the strangest thing — beside me is a round loaf of bread. I believe I am gone mad with hunger. I have seen men go mad like this. They see things that are not there.

I picked it up. It felt real. I tore off a piece and ate it. It tasted real.

I thought of Francis Collier. He says he tastes food in his dreams. This bread did not taste like a dream. I ate some more.

Now I must go on. I think I am halfway to the Indian village. I still do not know if the bread is real or not real. But I shall wrap it in my apron and take it with me. Even if it is not real, it tastes wonderfully good.

Later

I am not yet to the village. But I am so ill. I have found a big, hollowed-out log. I shall rest here a while. I still feel that eyes are watching me. I stop and look around. But there is no one. Not even deer or rabbits or wolves. Could it be the eyes of God? Or is it just fever?

I pray to Him to watch over me. And to forgive me for causing worry to Mama and Papa.

I shall sleep inside the log awhile. I do not even care about the bugs that I know must be there. I must sleep. I think I am burning up with fever. More later.

Later

When I awoke, I crept out from my log. And there — there were two Indian men looking down at me! My hand flew to my throat. My heart began thundering wildly in my chest. They looked so fierce, with their quivers of arrows and golden animal pelts hung about them. One Indian was very tall. The other was smaller with a twisted back. I looked hard at the smaller one. I knew him! He is called Rawhunt. He came to our fort with Pocahontas.

"Come," he said. He said it in our language, English.

I tell you, I thought, first dream bread. Now, dream Indians.

"Come," he said again. He pointed.

Then he set off, the other following. What could I do? I had to go along. Though I could see we were no longer following the river.

For a long time we walked, my heart thundering wildly. Where were they taking me? Did they mean me harm? No, or they would done the worst already. I believed they must be taking me to Pocahontas. I know that Rawhunt is a friend to Chief Powhatan.

Oh, yes, that must be where we go.

Later still

Oh, I am so full of hope. We are sitting on a log, resting before we go on. I think we shall be to the Indian village before dark.

When we stopped, I reached into my apron and took out my bread. It was swarming with little creatures. I did not care. I brushed them off carefully. Then I broke off some bread. I held out a bit to each of the Indians. They took it and ate it. So I know it is not dream bread. But I do not know much else. I feel swimmy and dizzy in my head.

The Indians stare at me as I write here. They peer over my shoulder and look at my book. I know they cannot read my words. But they make me anxious. I said to them, It is not polite to mind another's business. I do not think they understood my words. But they knew what I meant. They backed away.

Oh, I think I am wild with fever. Here I sit. In the forest. In the almost-dark. With two Indian men. And I am telling them to mind their manners. I must be truly mad.

They signal to me that we must go on. I shall write more later. If I am still alive.

Night

We walked a long, long way. Stars came out, and it became black in the woods. And still, we walked. And then, in the moonlight, I suddenly saw we were near the swampy land by the river — *our* river. We went on some more. And then I saw the fence. We were back at the fort! I was so angry. So disappointed. They had tricked me. They had led me home! Oh, I had not seen Pocahontas. I had not gotten food, but for this loaf of bread. I had failed in what I set out to do. I was so angry, I could boil. I am ashamed of this, but I sat down on the ground. And I pounded my fists into the earth.

Later. Much, much later.
But I do not know what day it is.

So much to tell about. Some I remember.
Some I do not remember, but Papa has told
me. I will try to tell about those things, too.
But I must do it in short, short spurts. Because
I am still very weak.

I am home safely now. That is the most
important thing to tell you. That and this:
Baby Abigail is crying loudly. I do think that is
the most pleasant sound I have ever heard.

That is all for now.

Next day

I am home, but Mama is not here. Papa
cares for me. Mama is hard at work at the sick
shed, Papa says. I asked for Mary. Papa says she
is well enough. But she, too, works daily with

the sick. I want to see Mary. But I *really* want to see Mama. I must know that she has forgiven me for running off.

Papa has forgiven me, I know. He called me Sweet Beth this morning.

So now I shall tell you what I can about my journey home from the forest. But can you wait till tomorrow? I am still so weak.

Morning

And now I come to the part that is so surprising that for a long time I thought I dreamed it. But I know now that I did not. It is this: The Indian men did not even wait for me when I stopped for my temper tantrum. They walked right on. I jumped up. I felt foolish. But then, something happened. I felt as though something struck me hard on my head. Everything became black around me. I stumbled and fell forward. And I do believe the tall Indian caught me up in his arms. Papa says I must have swooned from fever. And then, says Papa, the Indian man strode into the fort carrying me! He did. That was so brave of him. For the men here — the few left — they might have killed him. Papa says the Indian man laid me down gently. Then he motioned to Papa to look outside the gates.

And do you know what Papa found outside the gates? Oh, it is so delicious that I will keep you guessing. You will have to wait until tomorrow.

Next day

Was that mean of me to tease you like that? What Papa found were gifts. Fish. Bread. There was an entire slain buck. Even Papa says he thought it was all a dream. There is enough food now to keep us for days, perhaps even weeks. Perhaps it will even keep us till the supply ship comes — till Caleb comes. I am so happy. So relieved. But Papa seems deeply worried. I wonder why he does not rejoice more?

Now I will tell you a secret. I no longer feel so afraid to go out into the forest. I no longer feel so afraid of the Indians. Many of them are good and kind. Although I know this: Papa will slay me if I should ever do that again.

March 15, 1610, morning

I have looked at the marks Papa has made on the wall. I see that it is mid March. It is also five whole days since I left. Four whole days since I have returned. And still no Mama. Papa says she cannot leave the sick shed for even a moment. I do not understand why.

This morning when baby Abigail awoke, Papa laid her in my arms. She stared at me awhile. And then she began to wail. Oh, I was so happy! She seems a bit stronger. Later, Mistress Whistler came and took her away to nurse her. She has done this each day since I returned. Papa does not say so, but I believe Mama's milk has dried up from hunger. But poor Mistress Whistler has just had a baby. It was a little boy, but he was born dead. She has enough milk for now.

I do not much like Mistress Whistler. She is a silent, melancholy person, who rarely smiles or speaks. And when she does speak, it is often to say something bitter. Now, though, she is being generous. So why does that surprise me? I always think I have learned my lesson about not judging people. But I never do.

Later

I have slept all the afternoon! I want to get up. I want to go see Mary and Francis, and even little Amelia. Francis and Amelia are ill. But Papa says no. He has been at the sick shed all the afternoon. Now, he says I must rest on my pallet for at least one more day. And he forbids me to visit the sick shed. He says I might catch the disease.

But Mama is there. And my friends. And, besides, I have already caught the sickness. How much more could I catch?

Later still

Mistress Whistler has brought Abigail back home. I tried to pick her up, but my arms trembled. I am still too weak. I do not trust my arms. I just put my finger inside her hand. And oh, do you know! She grabbed it and held it tight!

March 16, 1610

Mama has still not come home to us. Today, I think I shall disobey Papa one more time. I will go to the sick shed. But I shall wait till Papa has gone about his duties. I must see my mama. I do not know why she has not come to me. Is she so angry with me?

Later

Mistress Whistler has again taken Baby Abigail. But Papa is still here. Why will he not leave? I wait and wait. Does he not have other work to do?

P.S. I just now hear Papa walking away down the path. I will make my way to the sick shed. I hope to make it back to bed before Papa returns.

March 17, 1610

Oh, why did Papa not tell me true? Mama is not tending the ill. She is ill herself. She lies on a pallet. Her eyes burn in her face. There are hot spots of fever on her cheeks. Mistress Whistler tends to her. Mary was there tending Francis and Amelia.

Mary and I held each other. There was no need for words. But that did not stop us. We talked and talked and talked.

We also cried. Fourteen people have died since I left — just five days ago. All of the Bridger boys have died, every single one!

There is not one of the family left but Mistress Bridger. I think Mary is sad about John, though she says not a word. I am sad for Mistress Bridger. How awful to lose your entire family!

Tonight, Papa found me in the sick shed. I told him that I would not leave my mama's side. He became almost angry at me. He said I was still too frail and weak. That is why he had not told me of Mama's illness.

He took my hand in both of his. He said, "I cannot lose you both."

I said, "She needs me, Papa."

He shook his head.

"I need *her*," I whispered.

He let me be.

March 18, 1610

Mama does not know that I am here. I sit by her side and sing to her. I dip cloths in water to cool her brow. Early this morning she opened her eyes a moment. I think then she knew I was there, for she smiled. And then she slept.

Francis Collier remains very ill, and so does Amelia. Amelia seems a bit better than Francis. But who knows? Sometimes those who seem the healthiest go right on and die. And the sickest ones get up and walk. I do not understand it. I just pray that Mama might live. I pray that they all might live.

March 19, 1610

Poor little Amelia. First her mama died, then her baby sister. And now her twin brothers have died, and her papa, too. I think she will recover, though perhaps not in spirit. She lies staring, watching us move around the sick shed. But she does not speak. Today, I had a thought. I hurried on home. I found the acorn dishes I had made and I brought them to her.

For the first time, she seemed to smile. She fell asleep, holding the tiny dishes in her hand.

Later

Today, Francis opened his eyes. I sat by his side and gave him sips of water, for his lips were parched. I told him that when he was better, I had some deer jerky for him. I have saved it. I will not touch it even if I am starving.

Francis nodded. His fingers fluttered. He

seemed to point at something. He fixed his eyes upon the ceiling. I could tell he wanted me to look up.

"What?" I asked.

I looked up to where he looked. I saw nothing. Nothing but rafters.

I looked back at him.

He was still looking at the ceiling.

I looked again. Just rafters. And some spiders in a corner. And — what else?

I looked back at Francis.

He was — gone. Dead. In that minute while I looked away, he died. I had let him slip away, and did not even watch him go. He went alone.

I cannot write more.

March 21, 1610, morning

This morning, Mary and I walked outside. We went to the edge of the woods. We listened to the birds and the rustling of the leaves. There are hints of spring in the air. I do not know why that makes me sad.

March 22, 1610, morning

There are at least ten bodies waiting to be buried. But there are few men strong enough to do it. There are only Papa and Master Collier and Master Dobson and a few of the stronger men who have somehow made it through this winter.

I think I am more afraid now than I have ever been. But I keep saying that, do I not?

March 23, 1610

This morning, Mary and I walked down to the main gate of the fort. Someone has left a note, scratched into one of the wooden posts. It tells that we are leaving this fort. It tells those in the supply ships to go north to look for us.

I do not know who has written those words. I know only that it makes sense. Perhaps we should all leave here. Perhaps we should all go and find a new place. We could join the Indians. But then Caleb would come and I would not be here.

I do not know. I think I am too weary to even think.

March 24, 1610

Oh, I do not understand. How can all this come to be? Mama has died. Yes. She has. She has slipped from life. I sat by her side and wiped her forehead. But I did not take my eyes from her face the whole morning. I would not let her slip away unnoticed as I did with Francis. But she still died, her eyes wide open. Oh, I pray she is seeing things in the next life that are happier than here. I hope she has food. I hope she meets Francis and those devilish twins. I pray that they talk and laugh. And . . . and I hope she will have new ribbons, and a new gown, and so much food, venison and cornmeal and honey and figs and dates and . . .

Oh, I am weeping. The page is wet.

More later. Perhaps.

Later

I wonder what is hope? There is no hope here. When I said that to Papa today, he only sighed. He did not even scold me. That is how bad he feels.

March 26, 1610

I do not mean to give up. I just get weary in my heart at times. But I know Mama would be unhappy with me for what I said. I shall try to be better. But I think of Caleb. He is coming here full of hope. But Mama is dead.

Weeks later

I have not written here in weeks. I cannot bear to. I keep thinking of poor Caleb. He is on his way now in the supply ship. He must be, for spring is here. He is sailing across that wide ocean. He is coming to us — to Papa and me and Abigail. And to Mama. But Mama is dead. I think his heart will break.

I know mine is broken.

Summer is upon us

The gates to the fort are always open now. We wander freely in and out. We no longer fear the Indians. What is left to fear? There is only death. I think we have become used to that.

But — Mary and I still talk. I still have a friend. We still dream. Yes, we do. Mary dreams of marrying.

I dream of my Caleb coming. And I dream of Mama.

I wonder why Mary seldom speaks of her

mother? Is it because she is older? Do you not grieve so much when you are thirteen or fourteen? I am only nine. I think I will grieve for the rest of my life.

June 10, 1610

Could it be? Could it be? Or am I dreaming? Mary and I sit by the river. I know there are sails far upriver. I saw them — huge sails of white, billowing in the wind. And then the mist came down. And they were gone. But for a moment, they were there. Were they not? Perhaps I am dreaming?

But Mary saw them, too.

Perhaps we are dreaming the same dream.

A few moments later

I close this book. I open this book. I pick up my pen. I set it down. We wait for the mist to clear. Mary and I clutch one another's hands.

Mary says it is real. And then she says, Food.

I say, Caleb.

She says, Raisins.

I say, Cornmeal. No worms.

Mary says, Stockings, petticoats, shoes.

I say, Ribbons for our hair.

We squint up our eyes and stare upriver. We wait for the sails to reappear. I still believe it is all a dream.

But then, why does Mary dream the same dream?

A minute later! Two minutes!

The mists have cleared. It is *not* a dream! Mary has run up to the clearing. She is shouting for everyone to come.

She runs back to stand next to me. Papa has come and is by my side. He holds Abigail.

Oh, glory, glory! It is a ship! It is so close.

Papa hugs me to him with one arm.

I am shaking so, I cannot hold this pen.

An hour or more later

The ship sails upriver. It comes close. So close. The sails billow and slacken. We see faces onboard. Caleb? Is my Caleb there?

Men are shouting from the ship. This glorious, glorious ship.

They throw ropes from the ship now, lowering things. A shallop glides toward shore.

Is he here? Is my Caleb onboard?

I cannot hold this pen. I must run and see. Is my brother aboard this glorious ship?

He is!

He *is!*

Late June, 1610

I have not written here in so long. Life is indeed like a hurricane aboard ship. It brings us up. It throws us down. We have food now. So much food, and so many rich supplies. The fort swells with strong, healthy people. There is a strong leader, Lord de La Warre. There are new children, boys and girls.

My Caleb is here.

But my mama is dead.

Oh, how Caleb grieved, we both grieved. Caleb had brought my journal, the one I sent to him. We are rereading it now. We are sharing all the things I have seen. We are reliving our times with Mama. I tell him how Mama missed him.

And oh, how Caleb loves baby Abigail. She is growing and wiggling about and trying to crawl away from us.

And something wonderful! When Abigail wants something, she howls!

July 1, 1610

You remember Mistress Whistler? Well, she is a widow woman now, as her husband died in the sickness. Sometimes I see her look at Papa in a certain way. It is the same way that Mary Dobson did look at John Bridger. Could it be? Caleb says no. But he does not know women as I do. Probably Papa does not know, either.

I know that we owe Mistress Whistler much, for without her, Abigail might have starved.

But I do not want her for a mama. She is still grim and cheerless. I believe I shall warn Papa.

August 11, 1610

It is one year today that we first set foot on this land. Here in my diary I have told you the story of the first year. Though parts of our story are sad, some are most joyous. The supply ship has brought most of our needs — food and medicines and strong new leaders and men and women and many children. The church bells ring daily, summoning us to prayer. Caleb has joined us here. We have built a house — a home — in Jamestown. We are at home in America.

And that, I think, is a glorious story.

P.S. Oh, and one more thing: All over the fort now, we hear children laughing.

Historical Note

In 1607, the London Company in England sent an expedition to America, with the express purpose of settling there and finding goods and materials to send back to England. In the spring, the ships arrived, then sailed up the James River where they settled the colony that came to be called Jamestown. Many of the colonists believed there was gold to be found in Jamestown that would make them, and the London Company, rich. Soon, however, it became clear that though there were many riches and good things to be found, gold was not one of them. Then, in 1609, new

James Fort.

ships arrived, carrying the first women and children, and thus overcrowding the fort. These newcomers had survived a terrible hurricane during the crossing in which several ships were lost, among them the *Sea Venture*. This ship carried many of the most essential provisions as well as instructions for who would govern the colony.

John Smith trading with the Indians.

For a time, there was much conflict about who would

lead. Eventually, however, a young colonist, Captain John Smith, took over the reins of the colony. He set down laws and fostered cordial relations with the Indians. But then, in the summer of 1609, Captain Smith suffered a serious accident that forced him to return to England, leaving the colony once again in turmoil.

The winter that followed was a desperate one for the colonists. Disease and hunger and starvation were their constant companions. Of the hundreds of settlers in the colony when Captain Smith

Among the many problems the colonists faced was lack of food.

sailed away in August of that year, only about sixty were still alive the following May when new ships arrived.

Lord de La Warre's ships meeting the colonists.

These ships had been built in Bermuda, reconstructed from the *Sea Venture* that had been shipwrecked. Some of the remaining colonists begged to be taken away, boarded the ships, and even began to sail down the river. But just as they arrived at the mouth of the river, they turned back, for

The House of Burgesses.

they had newfound hope. Three new supply ships were on the horizon, arriving from England. On board one was Lord de La Warre. He took over leadership of the colony. Under his strong guidance, and with the influx of healthy new people, and with food and medicines and supplies, the colony once more prospered. Church bells rang out; the fort was rebuilt; order was restored. Jamestown emerged at last, healthy and strong. It was named the first capital of Virginia. And in 1619, the House of Burgesses met there, the first representative legislative assembly ever to meet in the United States of America.

About the Author

Patricia Hermes is the author of over thirty five books for children and young adults including *Mama's Let's Dance*, *Cheat the Moon*, *Calling Me Home*, and a holiday series with Scholastic centered about another set of twins — Katie and her twin brother Obie. Many of her award-winning books have been named IRA/CBC Children's Choices, or awarded ALA Best Books.

As the mother of five children, her writing enables her to continue to heed the plea she heard so frequently from those children: Tell me a story.

Acknowledgments

The author wishes to thank the patient and ever-helpful research librarians and children's librarians in Fairfield, Connecticut.

Grateful acknowledgment is made for permission to reprint the following:

Cover portrait and frontispiece by Glenn Harrington.

Page 104 (top): James Fort, Colonial Williamsburg Foundation.
Page 104 (bottom): John Smith, Culver Pictures.
Page 105: Dealing out the five kernels of corn, Corbis-Bettmann.
Page 106 (top): Lord de La Warre's ships, North Wind Picture Archives, Alfred, Maine.
Page 106 (bottom): A representation of the first colonial assembly in Virginia in 1619; wood engraving, English, 19th Century. The Granger Collection, New York, New York.

For Madeline Victoria Hermes and Matthew Logan Hermes
Welcome to this new land!

⊰ ⊱

While the events described and some of the characters in this
book may be based on actual historical events and real people,
Elizabeth Barker is a fictional character, created by the author,
and her diary is a work of fiction.

Library of Congress Cataloging-in-Publication Data
Hermes, Patricia.
The starving time : Elizabeth's Jamestown Colony Diary, Book Two by Patricia Hermes.
ISBN 0-439-19998-0; 0-439-36902-9 (pbk.)
p. cm. — (My America)
Summary: Elizabeth Barker continues to write to her "friend," her diary,
as disease and lack of food further plague the suffering settlers at Jamestown.

1. Diaries — Fiction. 2. Jamestown (Va.). — History — Juvenile fiction.
3. Virginia — History — Colonial period, ca. 1600–1775 — Juvenile fiction.
[1. Jamestown (Va.) — History — Fiction.
2. Virginia — History — Colonial period, ca. 1600–1775 — Fiction.]
I. Title. II. Series.
PZ7.H4317St 2001
[Fic] — dc21   00-020200
CIP   AC

20 19 18 17   12 13 14 15 16/0

Display type was set in Caslon Antique.
The text type was set in Goudy.
Photo research by Zoe Moffitt
Book design by Elizabeth B. Parisi

Printed in the U.S.A. 23
First paperback edition, May 2002

⊰ ⊱